To Edward and Louisa A.S.

To Mum and Dad, with love L.H.

Published by
Lion Publishing plc
Mayfield House, 256 Banbury Road,
Oxford OX2 7DH, England
www.lion-publishing.co.uk
ISBN 0 7459 4588 0

First edition 2002
1 3 5 7 9 10 8 6 4 2 0

Typeset in 20/30 Goudy Old Style BT
Printed and bound in Malaysia

The Little Christmas Tree

The Little Christmas Tree

Andrea Skevington
Illustrations by Lorna Hussey

LION
Children's Books

Deep in the forest one dark night, it was so cold,
the stars were shivering in the sky.

Down below the stars, below the trees, a young rabbit peered out of his hole. He looked anxiously at the sky.

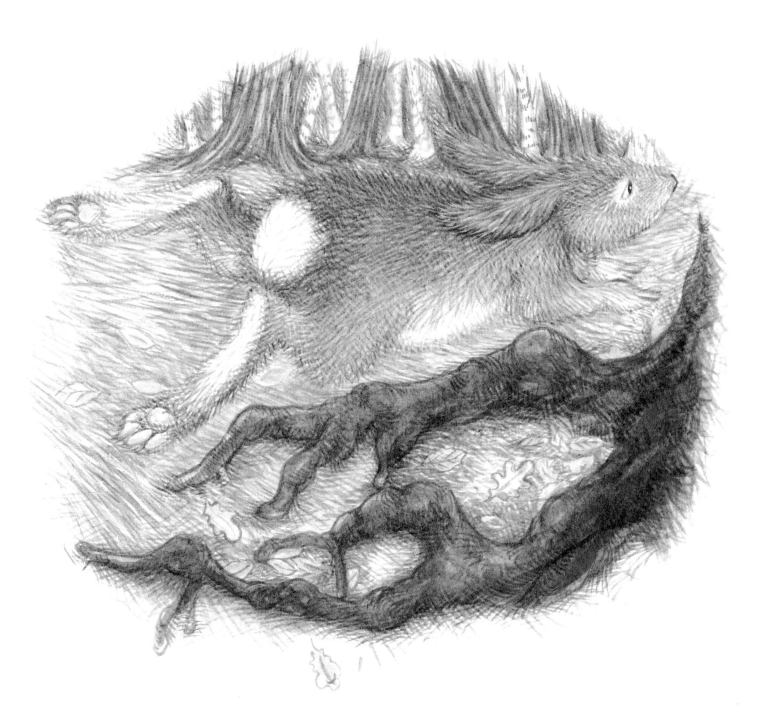

Little Rabbit could not sleep. Danger was coming,
he could sense it. His nose twitched this way and
that as he hopped from his warm home.

Badger stirred deep underground. He yawned
wide, then listened. The roots around him groaned.
A storm was gathering.

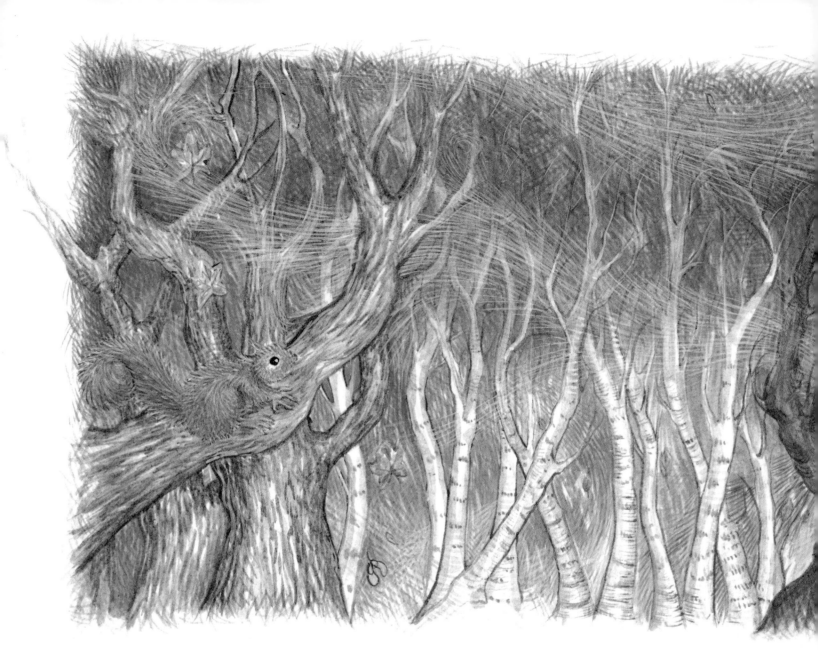

The wind crashed into the forest. Sycamores
clapped their bare branches together and sang how
beautiful and strong they were. The song was cold
and cruel. The massive oak spread wide, while the

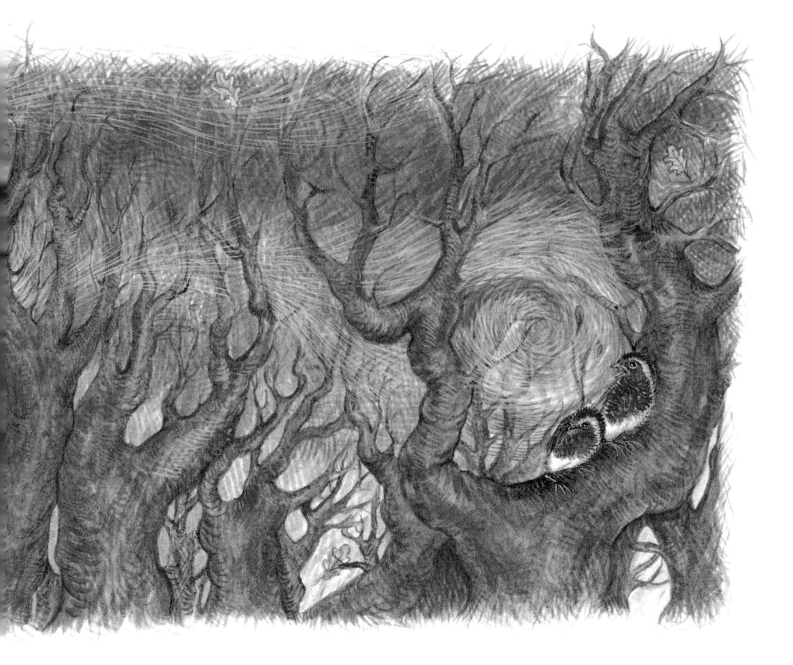

silver birches bowed and swayed in their winter
dance. But the birds clung to their nests and hid
their heads under trembling wings.

One tree did not join in. The Little Fir Tree stood alone, her heavy branches rustling on the forest floor. Her warm green leaves were still wrapped around her, while her soft voice sang gently. Her kind heart was full of love.

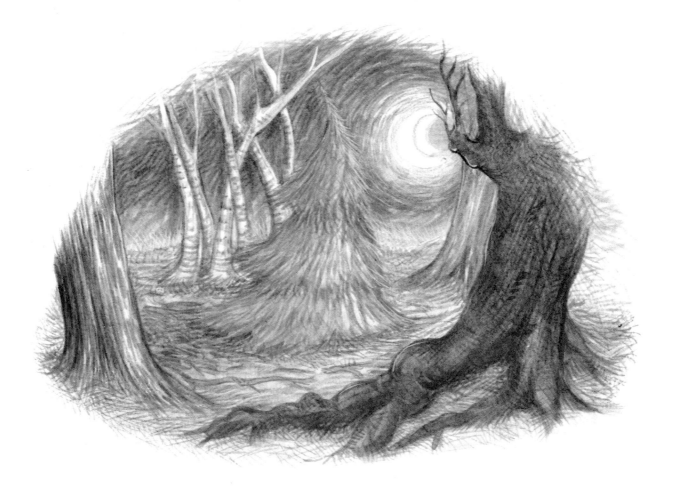

The other trees looked down and laughed. She was not like them.

Suddenly there was a loud CRACK! First one branch, then another, then another was torn from the trees in the forest.

Little Rabbit crouched low, his eyes wide.

The Little Fir Tree's leafy branches were tugged and bent low, yet she was not broken.

Badger crawled out of his ruined home. He looked up and saw the Little Fir Tree and smiled. She would shelter him. Little Rabbit shivered, all alone in the dark. But the Little Fir Tree bent her soft branches towards him and she brushed away his tears. Soon the birds came to her, for they had nowhere else to hide. She sang them a sweet lullaby, and even the wind hushed to listen.

Midnight fell in the still wood, and Little Rabbit
was the first to hear a new song – beautiful and full
of wonder. It grew louder.

He peeped from under the tree and looked at
the sky. It was filled with a pure, white light.

For far away, a baby had been born beneath a star,
while heaven's angels danced and sang for joy.

As the night sky grew dark again, stars from the angels' cloaks drifted down through the still air. One tall sycamore tried to catch them, but they were too quick.

The oak was sure they would land on him,
the king of the forest, but they slipped away.

A birch tree spread out her lacy twigs, yet the stars
tumbled on. They shimmered through the forest

until they found the Little Fir Tree, small and gentle,
with birds and animals gathered around her.

Like a soft fall of snow they covered the Little Fir Tree. All the animals gazed at the beauty of their little tree, and they heard her sing for joy.

So that was the first Christmas, when the sky was full of angels, and a mother laid her baby in sweet-smelling hay. And, still today, stars may fall on the place where there is love.

More Christmas books from
Lion Children's Books

Baboushka   *Arthur Scholey and Helen Cann*

The Christmas Play   *Clare Bevan and Julie Park*

The Christmas Sheep and Other Stories   *Avril Rowlands and Rosslyn Moran*

The Lion Storyteller Christmas Book   *Bob Hartman and Susie Poole*